Usborne
Little Wipe-Clean

Dinosaurs

to copy and trace

Illustrated by Jordan Wray

Designed by Jenny Brown

Words by Kirsteen Robson

Trace over the dotted lines for Stegosaurus and Triceratops.

Stegosaurus

Triceratops

Now trace the dinosaurs again
and copy the missing parts.

Trace over the dotted lines for Spinosaurus and Tyrannosaurus rex.

Spinosaurus

Tyrannosaurus rex

Now trace the dinosaurs again and copy the missing parts.

Trace over the dotted lines for
Diplodocus and Maiasaura.

Diplodocus

Maiasaura

Now trace the dinosaurs
again and copy the
missing parts.

Trace over the dotted lines for Iguanodon and Parasaurolophus.

Iguanodon

Parasaurolophus

Now trace the dinosaurs again
and copy the missing parts.

Trace over the dotted lines for Citipati and Therizinosaurus.

Citipati

Therizinosaurus

Now trace the dinosaurs again
and copy the missing parts.

Trace over the dotted lines for Pinacosaurus and Styracosaurus.

Pinacosaurus

Styracosaurus

Now trace the dinosaurs again
and copy the missing parts.

Trace over the dotted lines for Psittacosaurus and Protoceratops.

Psittacosaurus

Protoceratops

Now trace the dinosaurs again
and copy the missing parts.

Trace over the dotted lines for Muraenosaurus and Ophthalmosaurus.

Muraenosaurus

Ophthalmosaurus

Now trace the pictures again
and copy the missing parts.

Trace over the dotted lines for Ceratosaurus and Pachycephalosaurus.

Ceratosaurus

Pachycephalosaurus

Now trace the dinosaurs again
and copy the missing parts.

Trace over the dotted lines for Dimorphodon and Pterodaustro.

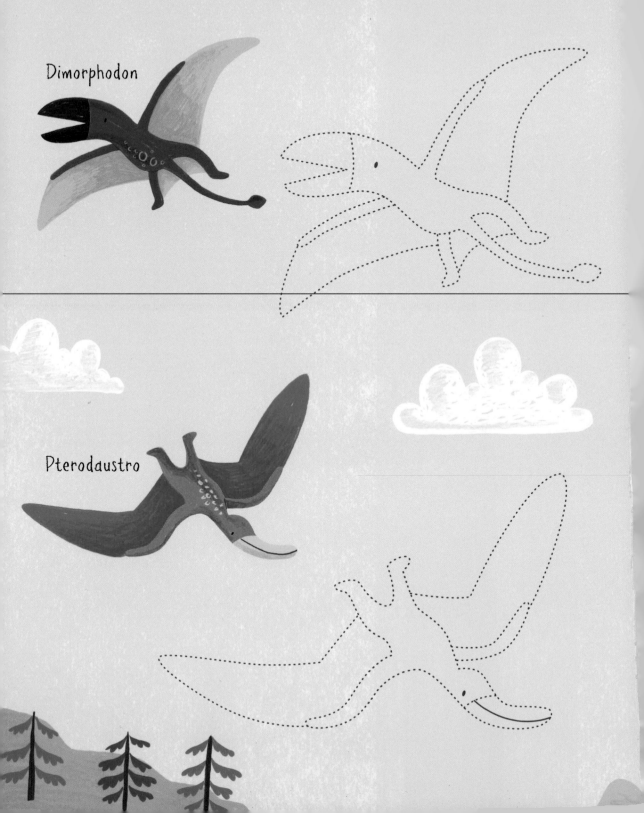

Dimorphodon

Pterodaustro